Polly™ and the Makeover Mess

Written by Pamela Jane
Illustrated by MADA Design, Inc.

© 2006 Mattel, Inc. and/or Origin Products Ltd.
The POLLY POCKET trademark is owned by Origin Products Ltd.
Other trademarks and trade dress are owned by Mattel, Inc. or
Origin Products Ltd. Manufactured under license from Mattel, Inc.
First Edition.
All Rights Reserved.

Manufactured and printed in the United States of America.
ISBN-13: 978-0-696-23189-6
ISBN-10: 0-696-23189-1

We welcome your comments and suggestions.
Write to us at: Meredith Books, Children's Books,
1716 Locust St., Des Moines, IA 50309-3023.
Visit us online at: meredithbooks.com

Meredith® Books
Des Moines, Iowa

Polly was planning a surprise.
"My cousin Pia is flying over from England on Saturday," she told her friends.
"I'm going to redo the guest room to surprise her!"

"Sweet! A room makeover. I'll help!" said Shani.

"Count me in," said Lila.

"Me too!" said Lea.

Polly's pals loved surprises, and Polly loved planning them!

Shani and Lila came over early Saturday morning to help Polly paint and hang wallpaper. Polly's dog Ollie relaxed on the floor.

"I'm all ready for work!" announced Lila, waving a set of paintbrushes.

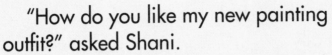

"How do you like my new painting outfit?" asked Shani.

"I love it," said Polly, "especially the crazy hat!"

"Lazy, daisy, crazy hat!" shouted Shani's parrot Rainbow.

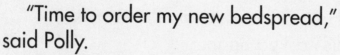

"Time to order my new bedspread," said Polly.

She looked around the room thoughtfully. "How about hot pink with black stripes?"

"Hot pink is way cool!" said Shani.

"Love it!" said Lila.

Polly picked up the telephone to order the new bedspread.

"You can deliver this afternoon? Perfect!" she said. "I'd like the hot pink bedspread with the black—"

Before she could finish, Lea breezed in with her new puppy Spots running ahead of her. Spots put his paws up on a table, almost knocking over the goldfish bowl.

Then he grabbed Ollie's favorite toy
and raced out the back door.
"Spots! Spots!" Polly and Lea called
after him.

Spots raced around the yard in circles,
dodging Ollie. The puppy was fast, but
Lea was faster.

"Got you!" she cried, grabbing the wriggling puppy.

"Whew! We better get to work," said Polly. "Pia will be here soon!"

Polly and her pals worked hard
all morning. They hung colorful new
wallpaper…

and painted trim…

and put up new curtains.

Finally they stepped back to admire their work.

"It's fantabulous!" said Shani.

"Practically perfect," said Lila.

"Polly-perfect!" squawked Rainbow, making everyone laugh.

"I can't wait to see Pia's face when she walks in!" said Polly.

"I wouldn't miss it for anything," said Shani.
"Me either," said Lea. "I'm going home to
get my camera. Come on, Spots!"

Spots leaped up, wagging his tail.
"Woof! Woof!"
"Spots, watch out!" yelled Polly.

It was too late! Spots had dipped his
tail into a bucket of black paint. He raced
around in circles, trying to see his tail.
"Spots, stop!" shouted Lea.

Spots stopped and shook himself briskly.
"Oh no, look what he's done!" cried Lila.

The four girls stared in dismay. Spots
had spattered big black spots all over the
brand-new wallpaper!
"Uh-oh," said Rainbow, shaking his head.

Samuel, the butler, poked his head into the room.

"I'd say this is a bit of a mess," he said.

"A bit of a mess? It's a major disaster!" wailed Polly.

"Pia will be here any minute. I wanted to surprise her, but not like this!"
Just then, the doorbell rang.
"Oh no, it's Pia!" said Lila. "What are we going to do?"

But it wasn't Pia. It was a deliveryman holding a big box.

"My new bedspread!" said Polly. "I almost forgot."

Inside the box was the new hot pink bedspread. Instead of black stripes, it was covered with big black spots.

"It matches the wallpaper perfectly!" said Lila.

"How did you know Spots would spatter black spots all over your walls?" asked Lea.

"I didn't!" said Polly.

"Maybe it's magic," said Shani.

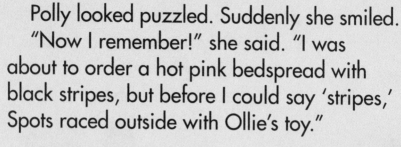

Polly looked puzzled. Suddenly she smiled. "Now I remember!" she said. "I was about to order a hot pink bedspread with black stripes, but before I could say 'stripes,' Spots raced outside with Ollie's toy."

"Then we yelled, 'Spots!'" added Lea.
Polly nodded. "So they thought I wanted
a pink bedspread—with black spots!"
Polly put the new bedspread on
the bed. The whole room glowed with
dazzling color.

"Wow," said Lila. "Pia's new guest room rocks!"

"I think I'll have Spots come over to my house and help me paint yellow spots on my wall," said Shani.

Spots wagged his tail, as if saying he'd be happy to help anytime. Then he ran to the door, barking.

This time it was Pia, just off the plane from England. She hugged Polly, then looked around the room with wide eyes.

"I say, what a super room! How on Earth did you paint all those fabulous black spots on the wall?"

"Well," said Lea, "it's a long story."

Shani nodded. "What a tale!"
Spots wagged his tail.

Polly giggled. "You mean, 'What a tail.'
Thank you, Spots!"

Fun Funky Fashions!

You too can add Pollyrific details to your own clothes! Try following these simple steps to add cool graphics to your jeans. Ask an adult for help if you need it. If you like the look, try it on a t-shirt too!

WHAT YOU NEED

Clean, dry, pressed jeans
Tracing paper
Pencil
Scissors
Fabric scraps
Iron
Fabric glue
Paintbrush
Tube of puffy or glitter
fabric paint

HERE'S HOW

1. Lay your jeans on a flat work surface. Draw or trace these flower shapes to the right or any other shapes onto tracing paper and cut them out. Place the patterns on scrap fabric, trace, and cut out the shapes.
2. Arrange the fabric shapes on your jeans. Use a paintbrush to spread an even amount of fabric glue on the back side of the fabric shapes. Press shapes onto the jeans, smoothing out any wrinkles.
3. Outline the fabric shapes using fabric paint. Let it dry.